This Book Belongs To

Name ____________________

Audio ISBN: 978-1-989264-01-0
E-Book ISBN: 978-1-989264-00-3
Print Book: 978-0-9808886-8-3
Published by Platinum Rouge
www.platinumrouge.com

Dedication

This book is dedicated with love, appreciation, and respect to my grandmother, Audrey Lambert, who raised me as her own daughter and who gave me memorable, bright, festive Christmases every year.

You spoiled me, treated me amazing, and always loved me. I love you too, and I will forever appreciate the sacrifices you made for me xo Jessie. Merry Christmas <3

"I believe that children are our future. Teach them well and let them lead the way. Show them all the beauty they possess inside."

Whitney Houston

Awesome Audrey's Kooky Christmas

Written By Jessica Lambert
Cover Art By Tredel Lambert

Far far away,
in the land of ABG,
lives the brightest
Christmas spirit,
in the form of a grannie.

Her hair is dusted grey,
and her back has a
slight hunch.

But boy does she love
Christmas; yes, she
loves Christmas,
a bunch.

Her name is Audrey Lambert, but the kids will always say, she's the ghetto's Santa, a.k.a. Awesome Audrey!

ABG is a land, where the rowdy kids play.

No one else will take them, so ABG is where they stay.

Audrey shakes her head, as she watches the kids run.

They don't know better, they find stealing fun.

Some do it for the candy, some do it for the clout.

Some do it for food to eat, they cannot go without.

“They won’t make
Santa’s list like that,”
Audrey chuckles away.

Then she starts back -
on another hardworking
day.

“Christmas won’t come
to the naughty or poor.

So I must plan for
Christmas, and then,
plan some more.”

Her jelly like belly

dances the Jingle Bell Rock.

As Awesome Audrey plans for Christmas,

right ‘round the clock.

She shops in the summer, spring, and fall.

Naughty and poor – yes, she remembers them all.

“No kid will be forgotten, not on my watch!

Let’s see, there’s Arabella and Kaidon; there’s Jessie and Lott.

There’s Teague and Nate, and my sweet boy Tre, who lives on the block - but is never naughty!”

ABG has kids with no parents, or maybe just one.

Kids whose parents are wacky and have too much fun.

Parents who hit, or who are down on their luck.

Parents who care, or some who don't give a duck.

ABG's struggle is real, but no one shows care.

Except Awesome Audrey – she's always there.

She hangs streamers on ceilings, and strings all the lights.

She lights the BBQ for marshmallows, and gives eggnog at night.

She makes the most magical cookies – the way only she could.

She made gingerbread ghettos – and da hood tastes darn good!

She makes peanut butter cookies, chocolate chip cookies, and macaroons.

She dances to Christmas carols.

She sings Christmas tunes.

The kids love Audrey, and she loves them too.

"Santa should have never forgotten about you."

Awesome Audrey writes Santa a "strongly worded letter" each year.

Reminding Santa that EVERYONE deserves Christmas cheer.

But Santa had gotten bidder. His heart had turned cold.

If Audrey was aging... Santa was ripe OLD!

Plus, he had a minor grudge, for no reason at all...

Okay, maybe he had a reason... but his reason was SMALL!!!

There was that one time... long, long ago.

Where Santa crashed into ABG land, needed help, and met Flow.

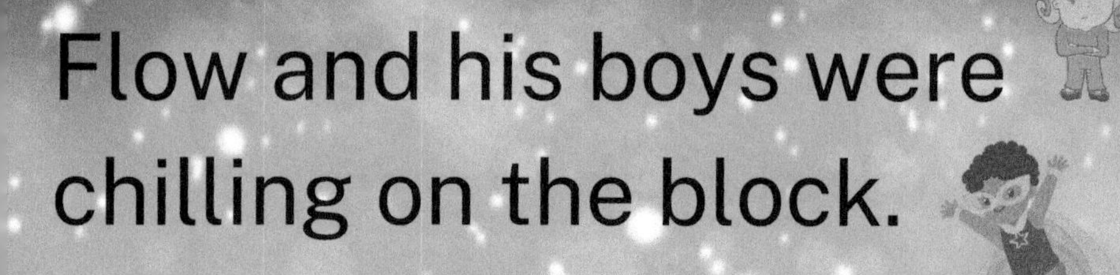

Flow and his boys were chilling on the block.

It was late at night, say 11 o'clock.

Santa asked directions, and Flow sang a song.

The kids of ABG land... well, it didn't take them long.

To run out singing,
headed right toward
Santa's sleigh.

Santa was stunned, he
didn't know what to say.

The sight filled Santa
with joy. His heart filled
with splendor.

Until Santa realized, his
situation was quite
tender.

The kids pushed over
Santa, and ransacked
his sack.

They took all his toys,
and wouldn't give them
back.

Santa cried for help,
but no one could hear.

They were all too busy,
stealing Santa's
Christmas cheer.

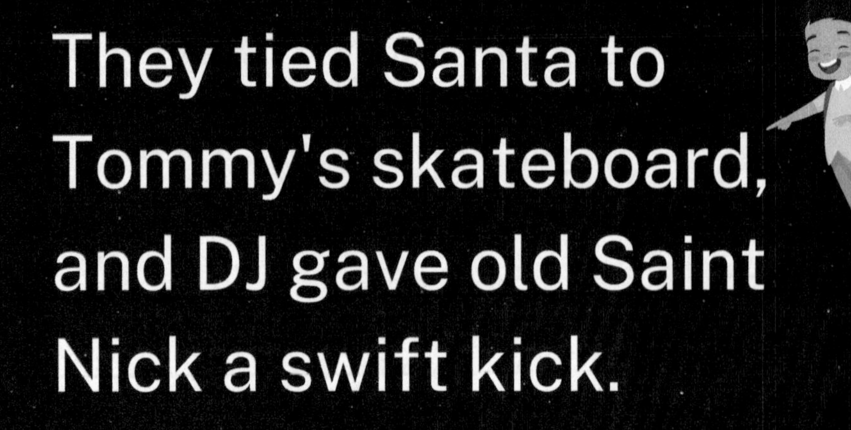

They tied Santa to Tommy's skateboard, and DJ gave old Saint Nick a swift kick.

"I don't like you Santa" said DJ.

"You can suck a sour stick!"

ABG kids laughed,

it served that fat man right.

He never gave them good gifts.

He always moved so tight.

Awesome Audrey
watched out the
window,

as all the others fled.

She stood there with
concern,

and simply shook her
head.

“Jessie – grab my scissors,"

she yelled up the stairs.

Her youngest daughter Jessie,

ran down, with two pairs.

“The red or the green Momma,

which would you like?”

“Oh, I don’t care Jessie.

It’s going to be a long night.”

Audrey grabbed the red and flew down the hall.

“Wait up” she could hear her sweet Jessie call.

Jess grabbed her flying board, all covered in foil.

It was make-shift and simple, but it slid just like oil.

Jump on Momma, Jessie grabbed Audrey's hand.

“Where to?” asked Jessie.

“The end of Burry Land!”

Jessie looked scared.

That was at the bottom of a hill, in a ditch!

Jessie peered over the iced cliff,

and saw Audrey free Saint Nick.

"Holey Moley"
Jessie cried.

She couldn't
believe her eyes.

"Holey Moley is Right."

Awesome Audrey
simply replied.

Santa looked mad.

His cheeks were red,
but not jolly.

“Now, now, Santa”
Audrey said.

“Remember to deck
the halls with holly."

"Bah-hum-bug"
Santa cussed.

His negativity
was hard to grasp.

"I hear by
banish Christmas!"

"For everyone?"
Audrey gasped.

This couldn't be true.

This had to be stopped.

Santa growled meanly,

"NO...Just for YOUR BLOCK!!!"

“You can’t do that”
Jessie cried.

“I can, and I have”
Santa defied.

Santa hopped on his
slay, still oh so mad.

“But I’ve always been
good. I’ve never been
bad.”

Jessie's tears froze while running down her cheek.

Audrey's heart broke, she could barely speak.

"But Santa" Audrey said, "some of these kids are good."

"I don't care," said Santa. "No more presents for the HOOD!"

Well, this made Audrey mad. Very mad indeed.

“You old lazy slob! You’re filled with hate and greed.

Your reindeer need a G.P.S.. They’re old, just like you!

Christmas used to be the best, now you don't have a clue.

"Mr. Santa,
you lost
your touch,
very long ago.

Now take your empty
sacks and mutts.

Get out of our ghetto!"
GET OUT!
OUT
ABG Tow

"MOMMA,"
Jessie was shocked,

and scared as could be.

"No Christmas Momma?

Ever?

Not for you?

Not for me?"

"Oh, we'll have
Christmas alright"
Audrey declared.

"The best you've
ever seen.

What do we need
this man for?

He's grumpy
and he's mean!"

"Santa who,"
Audrey laughed.

"Santa,
take a hike."

"Better yet,
you Santa fool,

go and
fly a kite!"

With that,
Audrey grabbed the cardboard in one hand,

and Jessie in the next.

“I have work to do now.

I will make Christmas the BEST!"

"I have helpers
who have chutzpah.

That is more
than I can say for you."

Audrey shook her head
at Santa.

“Old man,
you really
don’t have
a clue!”

She whisked away with Jessie on her cardboard,

and boy did they fly.

They were still on ground,

but it felt just like the sky.

They passed the
Flow man,

and Audrey gave
him a daps.

“Don’t worry kids”
she winked,

“that classist
won’t be back.”

The children's
eyes widened.

They were
clearly scared.

"No Christmas?
That's it?"

Now, it seemed
they cared.

Audrey gave a smile,
and sent them
off to bed.

The block was
quiet that night.

Audrey stayed up
to wrack her head.

“What will I do now?”
She said while all alone.

“I gave Saint Nick
the boot.

I sent Santa home.

I upset the reindeer,
they'll never fly
HERE again."

"I should have kept
my mouth shut.

Now, look what
I have done.

Everyone will hate me.

No more presents.
No more fun.

No point leaving
cookies - no Santa will
ever come."

"Man, I put my foot
in my mouth.

Yes, I really did it
this time.

I will need some
DOLLARS,

but all I have
are measly dimes."

Just then, Audrey heard the patter of little tiny feet.

Sherry and Jessie were up, looking for something to eat.

Audrey did not move, she just sat there with a frown.

Jessie and Sherry looked at her, two little angels in night gowns.

“Momma” Jessie said.

“Please don’t be sad. You’re worried about Christmas, but it won’t be bad."

Sherry stepped in, with wisdom of her own.

“We will help you Mrs. Lambert. You are not alone.

Truth be told, you’re the most festive person I ever knew.”

Sherry said, as she stood and watched Audrey stew.

“We believe in you Momma” Jessie assured.

Then, just like that, Audrey was cured.

Yes, Audrey felt a glow inside. One she hadn’t felt for a while.

She nodded her head toward the girls, with a reassuring smile.

“Okay kiddos,
it’s time for bed.

Let a party of
sugar plumbs,
dance in
your head.”

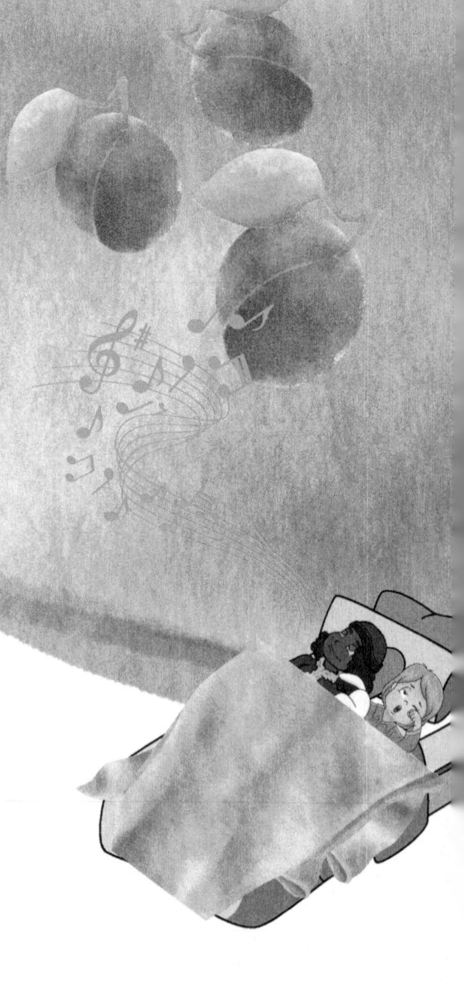

That night Audrey,

with her spirt anew,
forged the best plan
ever...

all she'd have to do,

is work day and night,

each and every day,

planning, decorating,
and maybe even pray.

The menu would be great.

She wouldn't serve up any beef.

Just oxtail with love.

Curried goat, bun & cheese!

She'd make a turkey too.

They could all watch it jive.

No, Christmas wasn't dead.

Because of Audrey, Christmas was more live.

She got her hood helpers,

who turned ABG into a winter dream.

It was always a party,

with the man-dem on the scene.

Prince and Nelly built a DJ booth and dancefloor that was as cool as could be.

They made it out of snow.

It went from ground to tree.

Milli spat on the mic,
with Nico by his side.

D-Money played a set.

Jen and Star slid
down the slide.

The boys started
a snowball fight,

that was really
quite fun.

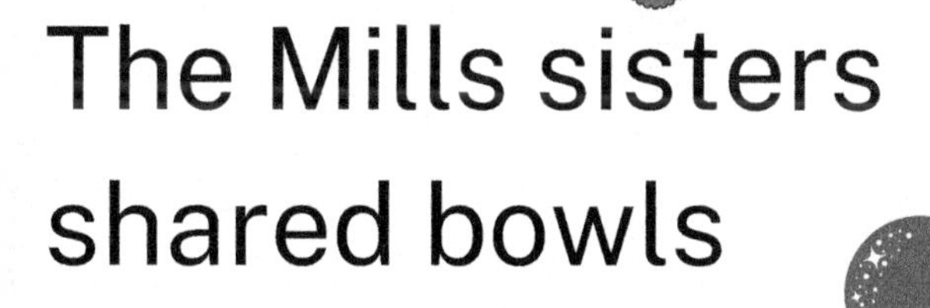

The Mills sisters
shared bowls

of maple snow
with everyone.

Tom found
a great BIG tree,

and decorated it
with lights.

It shone so bright,

you could see it,
‘roun the world,

when the other
side was night.

Lolla and Brit brought hummus to share.

Bianca and Bella danced without care.

The kids just kept coming. There were more and more.

Jessica, Mandy, Larissa, Brooklyn, and Lenore.

Ally, Ross, Dan, and Moe. Each so talented, it was quiet the show.

Cali, Nadia, and Arlene, rolled up with Flow Man on the scene.

The party bumped on the block so hard you could see,

the base booming across the entire city.

And the gifts - there were gifts - for every kid on the Mills.

There were gifts on rooftops. There were gifts up on hills.

There were gifts in the park, and in the yard.

There were gifts spread out wide, and gifts spread out far!

Where'd they
come from?

Well, that's not
the point!

They were gifts,
and they came.

It's not about who,
cased what joint!

Hood happy arrived,
and Santa was mad.

He tried to ruin
Christmas.

He tried to make them
sad.

He tried to punish them,
but he did not succeed.

Their Christmas
was jolly.

Red like bull,
green like tweed.

Their food was so yummy, you could still smell the pot.

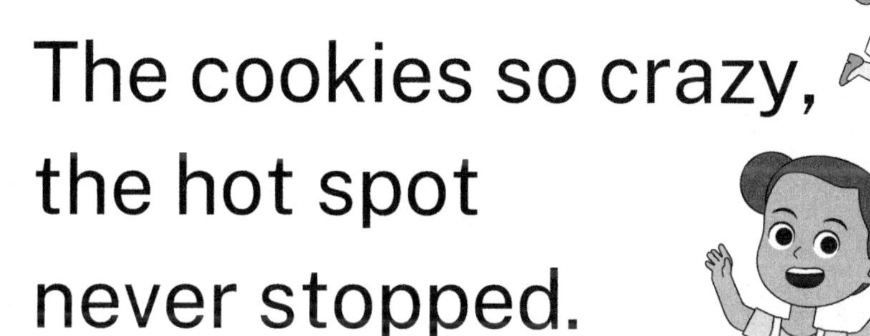

The cookies so crazy, the hot spot never stopped.

This ghetto outdid Santa. They outdid him indeed.

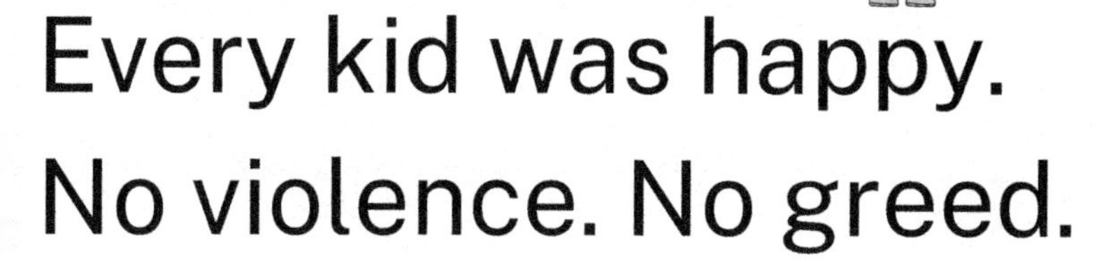

Every kid was happy. No violence. No greed.

The hood was
filled with love.

Yes, their groove
was getting on.

This was a Christmas
to celebrate.

Yes, Christmas had
them sprung.

Audrey laughed
and laughed,

from the comfort
of her chair.

Watching Jordan
and Jessie dance,

she loved what
she saw out there.

“You did it” whispered Audrey’s angel.

Her voice warmed Audrey’s heart.

“I knew you could” she said softly.

“I believed in you, from the start.”

"It's good" Audrey said. "A little crazy though."

Matt took her by surprise.

"Right-on, Durango!!!"

Audrey laughed and hugged Matt. He was her guy.

"A Christmas for champions.

Forget Santa, he’s fugazi.”

Audrey grabbed another glass of punch - singing

“Boom, boom, ain’t it great to be – crazy.”

That night,
the hood was
dark and cold,

but the fun never stopped.

Audrey found
some fireworks.

Then, she lit them up.

This Christmas
was one,
no other
could test.

Audrey was
feeling no pain,
singing
M.A.T.C.H.E.S.!

The hood was quiet
the next morning,

kids happy for
the time they had.

But saying goodbye
to yesterday,

was making them
a little sad.

"Christmas is not gone," Audrey said.

"It's only too-da-loo.

You will see it
in a while Crocodile.

Now, there's much work to do."

With that,

Audrey started toiling
for next year's big day.

While the kids
all smiled,

knowing more
good times,
were on their way.

That's how Awesome Audrey, became a hood celebrity.

You may love Santa,

but she's '*Santa*'
for the poor, forgotten, and "naughty!"

It’s easy to
praise Santa,

with his elves, reindeer,
and ‘nice list.’

But we love
Awesome Audrey,

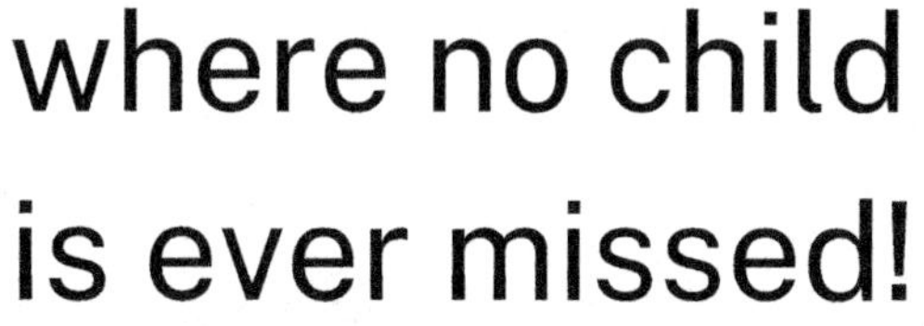

where no child
is ever missed!

In loving memory of Audrey Lambert (1930 - 2015)

Awesome Audrey is inspired by the magical spirt of a beautiful, kind hearted, and loving grandmother named Audrey Lambert.

Audrey loved Christmas so much that she kept her house decorated with streamers, and snowflakes, and reindeer, skating rinks, and Santa Clauses all year 'round.

Audrey lived in a winter wonderland, and shared her magic with all she loved and encountered. She had an open heart, and an open house. A real life earth angel, she touched many hearts, and changed the life of one very adorable little Jessie. This is Jessie's story.

ABG Land and the story of Awesome Audrey is created by Canadian Author Jessica Lambert. It weaves vibes from her childhood growing up in Toronto's Allenbury Gardens, and expands on her grandma's ability to make something out of nothing. Audrey Lambert created magical Christmases for those she loved, even during tough times. She really did shop summer, winter, and fall to make sure no child was ever forgotten!

Audrey Lambert, *a beautiful spirit in life, and in memory.*

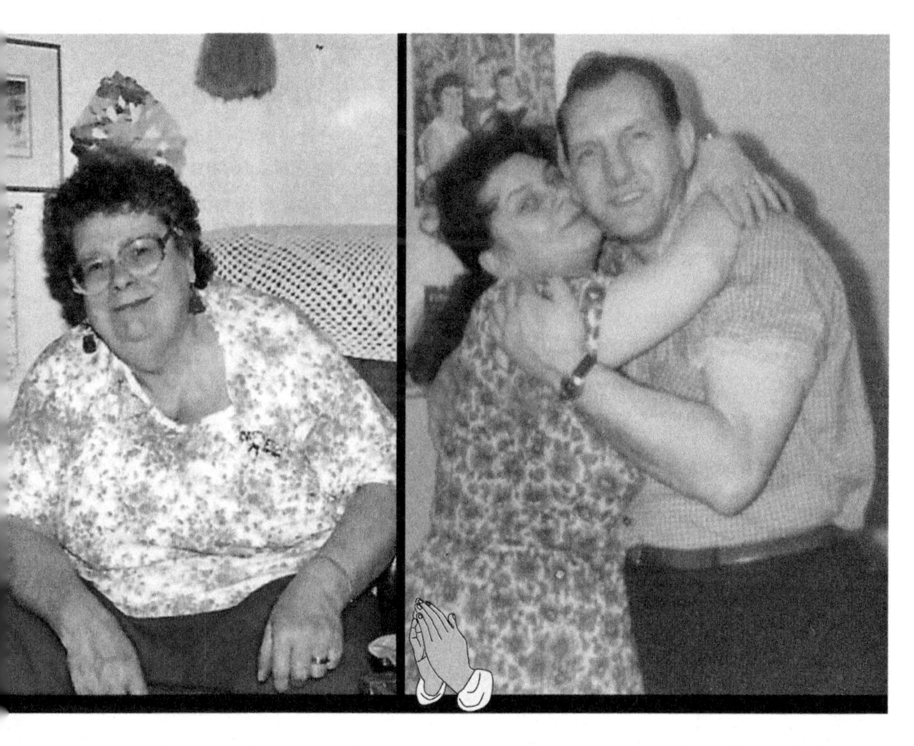

promised you this story, & I delivered.
I love you always grandma xo Jessie.

Honorable Mentions❤

This book was YEARS in the making. My grandma passed away in 2015 but her spirt lives strong through this story and her love. I promised her this book, my son Tredel has supported the process the entire way and even illustrated the cover and created the characters Jessie and Awesome Audrey. Tre is creating a fully illustrated edition which I am excited about. Thank you Tredel the Comic God for helping me tell a great story, and for helping to bring it to life with real characters. Thank you to my mother Heather Lambert who was the first to hear the story after Tredel and who supported me whole heartedly. Thank you to Tyrone for always having my back and standing by my side no matter the venture or adventure. Thank you to CJ and Larry who I so sheepishly read the story to, scared to get the ABG stamp of approval - the love, inspiration, and encouragement you BOTH gave me means the world to me and I love you both very much. Shout out to my fam Snow (Darrin), your energy adds something special to our neighborhood's legacy. Much love to Rolla, Sonia, Osama, Anwar and my sister Trecia you guys are foundation and I am grateful I got to experience childhood with you. Tim, my uncle raised as my bro, I love you so much - thanks for continuing to be the festive glue in our family. Scottie thanks for being a great big cousin - holidays were the best when you were there. I love ALL my little cousins - a special shout out to Jaguar, Sunny, Julia, Jasmine, Paige, Luke, Rob, Zach, and Caitlin. While this book was based on the spirit of my grandma, and her love for Christmas, there are elements of old-school FAM that make this book special. We boosted each other. We will always share the magical memory of growing up in ABG. Big up Eileen, Iva, April, Ruby, Yevel, Nadine, Michelle, Tony, Seaton, Kevel, Tristin, Jude, the Evans, Burgess, Bonds, Peters, O'Briens, Prettys, Bennetts, Mills', Reddons, Piticcos, Talanis, Scotts, Pattersons, and Ugwuegbulas, Collin, Alison, Kenton, Garth, Mark, Chelsie, Juliette, Tammy and my brother Donmillion (Randy) I can't cover everyone but I love you all. In loving memory of Amy Davidson, Sherry Monk, and Bill MacKay. To my bestie Stacey you are so special to me. To Devo, Brooklyn, Luna, Rashad, Jad, Marcus, Savs, Ryker, Evelyn, Matt, and my God Children Chanelle, Alexis, Keith, Nathanial, Steven, Christopher, Kaidon, and Teague I love you.

About the Author ~

Jessica Lambert grew up in Toronto, Canada with her grandmother Audrey, and her uncle Tim.

Today, Jessica is a the proud mother; her son is the talented Illustrator, Tredel the Comic God. Tredel Lambert.is also Jessica's business partner and co-Author.

Jessica is a Communication's and Business Specialist. She is also the Host of Jessie's World podcast - a podcast that helps people become their best selves, and the co-author to children's book series *Hip Hop Heroz* which helps children learn life-skills and includes published titles *Jack Fly*, and *No Chainz*.

Jessica has published several books, short stories, songs, and poems for children and adults. With a background in casting, and experience judging talent shows, hosting, and managing various events, and running a successful Talent Agency - Jessica is an entertainment guru who loves all things CREATIVE!

Jessica continues to create books, stories, poems, podcasts, platforms, products, and productions. She is co-owner of Platinum Indie, a platform dedicated to helping Indie Recording Artists, Labels, and Managers win BIG!

An experienced public speaker, facilitator, and business & life success strategist, Jessica is available for bookings and can be contacted via **Instagram @jessicavibez** or by emailing platinumrougemedia@gmail.com .

Platinum Rouge Titles

No Chainz - Hip Hop Heroz

Jack Fly - Hip Hop Heroz

Kiki's Pet Rock

Snow Sisters

Amanda Mae Minds Her BizNiz

Popstar Song Journal

Rap Lyrics Journal

platinumrouge.com

Printed in Great Britain
by Amazon